To Vicki with the laughing eyes - you always believed. And to my wonderful daughters, Heidi and Haleigh. May your lives be full of trust and adventure!!!

Mark Henn is a true man of God whose talent is one in a million, as evidenced by his many animated characters for Disney. His work so capably brings clarity to each page of this story. I am so grateful for the relationship that has been forged through the collaboration of this, our first book. May it be the first of many, and may our Father God bless this effort for His Kingdom.

Daniel Holom

Copyright© 2008 Daniel Scott Holom and Mark Henn

Library of Congress

ISBN 978-0-9845752-0-6

Printed in the United States of America

Sleepy Sheepy®
and Daniel

A long time ago, when King Darius
ruled over Babylon, a man named Daniel
loved and served God with all his heart.
He also served
the King.

1

Daniel wanted to do what was right and spent a lot of time asking God to show him the best way.

Three times every day, Daniel walked up the steps to his room and knelt to pray.

"I can't imagine who he talks to, Sifter," said Sleepy Sheepy, a small fluffy lamb. "Is somebody up there?" Sleepy was curious and full of questions.

Sifter, being a wise old horse, didn't get frustrated when Sleepy asked him about things. "Well Sleepy, Daniel talks to . . ." he was interrupted when the door at the top of the stairs swung open with a creaky, groaning squeak.

"Good morning dear friends," Daniel sang as he bounced down the steps. Tenderly he patted the horse's neck, and then reached up to scratch his ears. "Sifter, are you taking care of your younger stablemates? They need your wise advice. And Sleepy, I hope you're watching and learning from old Sifter." Turning around, Daniel called, "Coco! Oh, Coco, are you hiding again?" Daniel chuckled as a long-legged camel jumped out from behind a large pile of hay. "Coco! You get me every time!" He lovingly patted the camel's nose.

With a sigh, Daniel looked around his little stable. "Well friends, I wish I could stay and chat with you longer, but I must get to the palace. The King is depending on me this morning."

As they did each day
when Daniel went to work,
the animals waited until the
echoes of Daniel's footsteps
faded into the noisy streets of Babylon before they crept
out of the stable door.

They loved their master so much that
they wanted to be near him.
They had discovered a small
alcove near the
King's
quarters
that allowed them to watch
and listen as Daniel advised
the King.

One night when Daniel was working late, the
animals noticed three men lurking behind a
pillar as they eavesdropped on Daniel
and the King's conversation.

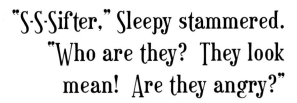

"S-S-Sifter," Sleepy stammered.
"Who are they? They look
mean! Are they angry?"

"Maybe their mother made
them eat broccoli for dinner,"
said Coco. Sleepy giggled.

"No Coco," Sifter said,
"those men are advisors to
the King, just like Daniel.
Some of the King's advisors are becoming jealous of Daniel
because the King listens to Daniel's advice and not to theirs."

Sleepy slowly nodded his head, not quite sure he understood.
"It's more fun to imagine them eating broccoli," Coco said.

That night, the animals quietly followed Daniel as he made his way through the streets of Babylon.

When they reached their cozy stable, Sleepy watched as Daniel's door closed and a light came on in the window. He could see the shadow of Daniel kneeling in the room. "He always does that when he gets home. And I can't imagine why."

"It makes him happy. I've seen the smile on his face," said Coco.

Sifter nodded. "It's the most important thing to him."

The next day, the animals were watching Daniel meet with the King; when suddenly, the three men slinked into the room, standing close enough for Sleepy and his friends to overhear them plotting.

"Emu!" Hackle hissed.

"Yeah Hackle?"

"You and Tell-All listen real close to see if we can catch Daniel lying. If we can, then the King will get rid of him, and we'll be his most important advisors." Hackle rubbed his hands together and laughed slyly.

Sleepy Sheepy's eyes flew wide open. "Oh no!" he whispered to Coco. "Those guys are trying to hurt Daniel." But Daniel had done nothing wrong.

The three scheming men hid behind the column for a long time. But as Daniel's meeting with the King went on, they began to get uncomfortable.

"Uh, hey Hackle, there isn't nothin' he said that's bad. Right? Am I right Hackle?" Tell-All bounced up and down as he asked.

"Yes, you're right," Hackle growled.

"But there's got to be *something*. Isn't there something he does that we can use against him?" Emu asked, fists clenched.

"I'm not sure," Hackle said slowly. Hackle's face suddenly brightened and he stuck one finger up in the air. "Wait a minute! Maybe there is!" Hackle put his arms around his two friends' shoulders and began to whisper. The other two nodded and laughed as Hackle told his plan.

"That's great, Hackle!" said Emu, a little too loudly.

"Shhhh!" Hackle and Tell-All warned him.

"That's great, Hackle," Emu said in a whisper. "That's why you're our leader!"

The three spent the night hatching their wicked plan, and the next morning presented it to the King.

Bowing low, Hackle greeted the King. "Oh glorious King, we suggest that you sign into law that everyone should seek help *from only you*. No one should be allowed to ask God for help for the next 30 days. If you disobey, you will be thrown into the lion's den."

The King's face began to glow with pride as he thought of this new law. "Yes," he replied with satisfaction. "That sounds very good indeed!

Yes! I'll sign it! Bring it here at once, Hackle."

As Hackle walked toward the throne, the animals watched from their hidden alcove.

"That's a trick!
Don't do it!"
Sleepy Sheepy bleated.
But the King didn't
understand sheep.

"It's a lie!"
Coco bellowed.
But the King didn't
understand camel.

"They only care about themselves!"
Sifter whinnied loudly. But the King didn't
understand horse. He signed the new law.

That night the animals stood warm in their stable munching their dinner when Daniel's aide ran breathlessly into the courtyard.

He bounded up the stairs and pounded on the door. As it opened, the animals overheard the aide say, "You won't believe what's happened! The King has signed a new law ..." The words disappeared as Daniel's door closed.

"I still don't undertand," said Sleepy. "Why would the new law be bad for Daniel?"

Sifter looked at Sleepy. "My young friend, that law is treacherous for Daniel. Do you know who he talks to when he kneels?" Sleepy shook his head. "The living God," Sifter explained. "He prays three times a day to God to seek His help."

"But if he prays to God, isn't that against the law? Won't he get thrown into the lion's den?" Sleepy shivered with fear when he thought about the lion's den.

"Yes," Sifter's gentle eyes shone with confidence. "But Sleepy, Daniel will not abandon his greatest friend. He trusts God!"

"Oh no, Sifter. If Daniel seeks God's help, he'll be thrown into the lion's den. Then we'll lose our dear master forever! How can his trust in God help him then?" Sleepy began to whimper.

Suddenly, Coco gasped, "Hey! Look you guys! Daniel's praying again!" They all looked up to see the shadow of Daniel kneeling in his room, but they also saw another shadow tiptoeing up the stairs and stopping to peer into Daniel's window.

"Wh-wh-who's that, Sifter?" Sleepy stammered as he once again began to shiver in fear. Then the small figure dressed in all black slipped down the stairs and out onto the street.

"That's Peccary, the spy!" Sifter said with surprise. "Those three mean men must have hired him to catch Daniel breaking the King's new law!"

"Oh no," moaned Sleepy and Coco together. "We've got to stop him!"

The animals scrambled to follow Peccary, but froze in fear as Hackle, Emu and Tell-All ran into the courtyard.

"Climb these stairs and look through that window," Peccary hissed. "You will see exactly what you need to see."

At Daniel's window, the three men quietly peered at the praying figure inside.

"Perfect," said Hackle and he and the other men hurried up the street.

"Oh dear, oh dear, oh dear," wept Sleepy. "See! I told you Daniel's trust in God would not save him!" Sleepy shivered under his woolly coat.

Sifter bowed his head low and looked intently into Sleepy's eyes. "Listen to me, young one. God is more powerful than those evil men. Let us trust in God as our master does. Now, let's hurry and follow those men and see if we can help Daniel."

With heavy hearts, the animals ran through the streets. Sleepy tried as hard as he could to trust God, but he wasn't sure what that really meant. "What can God do once Daniel is thrown into the lion's den?" he sobbed. His little heart almost broke.

By the time the animals got to the King's quarters, it was too late. From their hiding place, they watched as Hackle unfolded the signed law.

"You understand, oh wise King," Hackle announced smoothly, "that once a law is established, even you cannot change it. And punishment must be given to those who break the law."

"Daniel continues to pray to his God.

We have seen him with our own eyes."

"Oh no," wailed the King, "not Daniel!" The King wanted to save Daniel's life, but he could not change the law.

So he sent soldiers to have Daniel arrested.

The sad animals watched as Daniel was led to the lion's den. The King also watched, feeling foolish for the law he had made.

He could not rescue his dear friend.
"Daniel," the King called out,
"your God will
deliver you!"

Then Daniel was thrown in with the hungry lions.
The soldiers locked the door to the den.

"I hope his God saves him," whispered the King as he turned and rode back to the palace.

"Oh Sifter," whimpered Coco. "Isn't there anything we can do?"

Sleepy sniffled as he looked to the wise old horse. "Yes Sifter. Can't we do something?"

"I'm not sure. All I know to do is trust in God, as Daniel has shown us."

As three sad friends trudged toward the locked opening to the lion's den, they could hear the ferocious growling of the lions inside. Sleepy shivered in fear. "Oh, that horrible roar!"

"Hey! What's this?" He saw a tiny crack in the door to the den. "I can see inside!"

"What? What do you see?" Sifter demanded.

23

"Daniel is kneeling.

And the lions
are furious!

They're circling around him,
but they're not attacking. Wait!
There's someone else in there! He's gigantic!

He's actually closing the mouths of
the lions!"

Meanwhile, back in the palace, the King was not getting a wink of sleep.

He was worried about his friend Daniel.

At the break of day, he ran as fast as he could to the lion's den.

Breathless, he fell to the ground.
With a raspy voice he asked, "Daniel!
You serve the living God.
Did He rescue you?"

Daniel smiled and called out,
"The lions' mouths were shut by an angel! I'm not harmed!"

The King was overjoyed and gave the order for Daniel's release. There was not a scratch on Daniel's body!

"That was remarkable!" said Coco.
    "That was incredible!" said Sifter
"That was amazing."
shouted Sleepy.

"Daniel's trust in God really *did* help him!
God really can help us if we trust him!"
Sleepy was ecstatic.

Sifter chuckled. "You're right little one.
Now you understand."

The three turned around and hurried after
Daniel and the King who were already
walking toward the palace.

Hackle, Emu and Tell-All weren't as excited about Daniel's rescue.

King Darius had everyone who had plotted against Daniel thrown into the lion's den. And the angel of the Lord did not protect them.

That evening, as Daniel's shadow knelt in the room above their stable, Coco, Sifter and Sleepy Sheepy bowed their heads, too. "Thank you God, for protecting our master," prayed Sifter.

"And thank you for teaching me about trusting You," prayed Sleepy. "Please help me to trust you like Daniel does."

And do you know what? God helped Sleepy do just that.

SLEEPY SHEEPY AND DANIEL©

Storyboard:

Artist and writer have brought to life the historic story of Daniel, a Jewish captive, taken by Nebuchadnezzar to Babylon in 605 B.C. Although an outsider from ancient Jerusalem, Daniel experienced the most unlikely rise to power within the ranks of governors and commissioners. King Darius, Nebuchadnezzar's successor, began organizing his government. He planned to appoint Daniel over the entire kingdom. The other two commissioners and the 120 governors would be required to answer to Daniel. All went well, until one dark night when three of the King's advisors secretly listened to a conversation between King Darius and Daniel. Suddenly everything exploded, circumstances accelerated out of control.

Watch the astounding turn of events. See what happens when jealousy, hatred and betrayal enter the scene. Would there be a rescue? Was this the end, or was it only the beginning? Discover with Sleepy Sheepy™ the true secret in Daniel's life. Enjoy the humor of Coco the Camel, and the wisdom of Sifter the Horse.

About us:

MARK HENN, one of Disney's *best* animators, 1980 - present; works out of the Burbank, California Disney Studio. The following is a list of characters Mark has animated: Young Simba "Lion King"; Mickey Mouse "in several projects"; Goofy; Basil and Dawson "The Great Mouse Detective"; Oliver and Dodger "Oliver and Company"; Bernard and Bianca "The Rescuers Down Under"; Grace the Cow "Home on the Range"; Ariel "The Little Mermaid"; Jasmine "Aladdin"; Belle "Beauty and the Beast"; Mulan "Mulan"; Pocahontas "Pocahontas"; Giselle "Enchanted." He has recently completed work on Princess Tiana in "The Princess and the Frog." Currently he is working on the character Winnie the Pooh in an animated feature due in theaters the Summer of 2011. Mark also directed the award-winning short feature, "John Henry, Steel Driving Man."

Mark lives with his wife, Debbie, in southern California. They have two grown children.

DANIEL HOLOM, Senior Vice President - Investments, Financial Advisor, Wells Fargo Advisors, LLC. Daniel began his career as a Financial Advisor in 1983 and continues to this day. He is a graduate of Olivet Nazarene University with a degree in English Literature. He has spent many years volunteering in public service, and caring for those less fortunate. Through this, a passionate vision emerged of producing something with lasting influence.

Daniel lives with his wife, Vicki, and their two daughters in central Arkansas.

You can contact Daniel at (501) 851-7741.